DAKOTA'S MOM GOES TO THE HOSPITAL

by
Annie Thiel, Ph.D.

illustrated by
William M. Edwards
and
Karen Marjoribanks

PLAYDATE KIDS PUBLISHING
LOS ANGELES

A PLAYDATE PUBLICATION

For my grandchildren Brian, Mary, Matthew, Seth, Owen and Clara
and to all the children I've helped for the past 34 years in Malibu, my hometown - A.T.

For Julian - W.M.E.

Contents © 2006 Playdate Kids Publishing
Story Concepts © 2006 Playdate Kids Publishing/Interpath Inc.
Second Edition

PO Box 2785
Malibu, CA 90265-9998

ISBN-10: 1-933721-26-X
ISBN-13: 978-1-933721-26-2

Library of Congress Control Number 2007926211
SAN # 6300065

Printed in Korea

Before school, Dakota's mom would open the curtains to let in the sunshine.
"Wake up, Dakota," she would say, kissing Dakota's cheeks.

Mom would make a big breakfast...

...help her get ready...

...make sure she left on time...

...and pack the best lunch.

One day, Mom said she was not feeling well.
"I'll call the doctor," said Dad.

Mom was really sick and needed to go
to the hospital right away.

"Why did Mom have to come here?" Dakota asked Dad.
"I don't like the hospital. It's scary."

"There she is!" Dakota said.
"But why is she asleep?
And what are all those machines doing?"

"She might look different because of the medicine, but she's still your mom, and she still loves you!" Dad added.

While Mom was in the hospital,
Dakota tried to help by doing things on her own.

But she still missed Mom in the morning when she woke up.

She missed Mom when she was getting ready...

...when Dad tried to make breakfast...

...when Dad packed her lunch...

...and when she wasn't always on time.

13

After school, Dakota saw other kids
playing in the park with THEIR moms.
She felt jealous.

At home, Dad didn't do things the same way Mom used to.
Dakota felt angry.
"WHY does Mom HAVE to be SICK!" she yelled.

Dakota tried using her words, and talked to Dad one night.
"Why did MY Mom have to get sick?" she asked.

"It's hard to tell," Dad said.

"You might feel lots of things while Mom
is in the hospital," Dad said.
"It's okay to feel scared, confused, sad or mad."

Scared

Confused

Sad

Mad

"Just remember to talk to someone you trust
about your feelings, like me or Grandma."

Dakota and Dad thought of fun things to do together in between visits to Mom.

Even though Dad didn't do things the way Mom did them, he always made Dakota feel special.

One night, he made his yummy spaghetti.
"My favorite!" Dakota said.

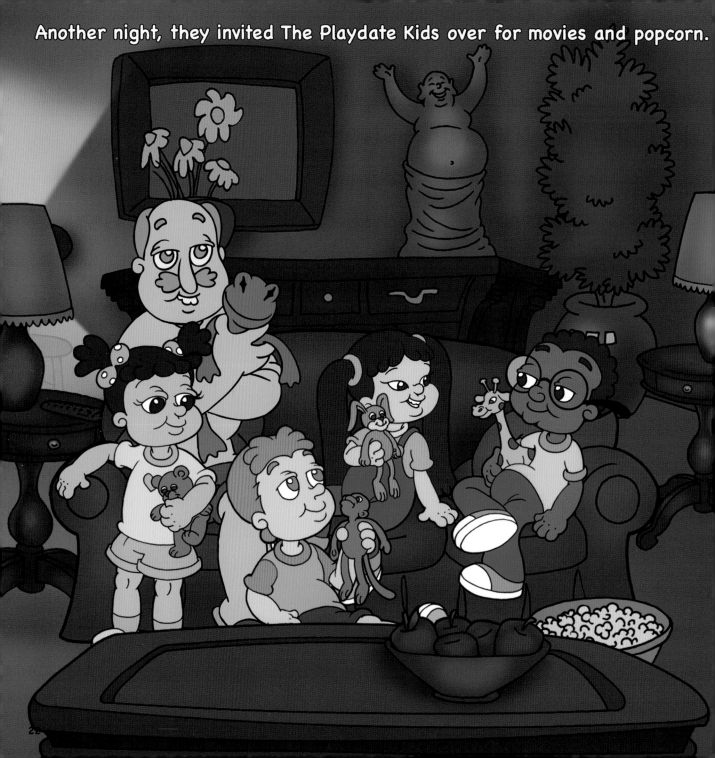

Another night, they invited The Playdate Kids over for movies and popcorn.

And every weekend, Dakota and Dad rode
their bikes around the neighborhood.

After a while, the doctors said Mom was well enough to come home.
Dakota was so happy!

24

"Look, Mom!" said Dakota.
"Dad and I made you a banner!"

"We're glad you're feeling better," Dad said.

Dad and Dakota still had to take care of Mom until she was strong enough to take care of herself again. But it was great to have her back home.

Dakota's Mom got better, and everything
was just as it used to be, except for one thing...

"Dakota, you've helped so much," said Mom.
"You've really become a big girl. I love you."
"I love you too, Mom," said Dakota,
and she knew it was true.

27

THINGS TO REMEMBER WHEN SOMEONE YOU LOVE IS SICK

1. Write them a letter or make them a special drawing.

2. Visit them in the hospital and sit with them.

3. Talk to someone you trust about your feelings. It's okay to feel sad, mad or even jealous of other families.

4. Put together pictures of the two of you and make a special album to share with them. Bring them photographs of home to keep with them in the hospital.

5. Are there things you can do all by yourself? Talk to an adult about ways you can take care of yourself.

6. Help by doing some of their chores for them while they are too sick to do them.

7. At home, help bring food and water to the sick person. Read aloud to the sick person if they are too tired.

8. Remember, nothing YOU did made your loved one sick. Doctors can help people feel better, but sometimes they don't even know why people get sick.

9. Be cheerful when they are awake, and quiet when they are sleeping.

10. Always tell them you love them!

SUPER COOL
STUFF TO DO

Pick some pretty flowers from your yard, or buy some at the market, and make a bouquet. Take them to the hospital and give them to the person you love.

If the person is in a special part of the hospital where they do not allow flowers, draw a picture of flowers instead.

Make a "Welcome Home" banner for when your loved one comes home. Put decorations, pictures, or flowers in their room to make it more cheerful.

When your loved one feels like having visitors, invite friends and family to come to your home. Get an adult to help you bake cookies to serve to guests when they come to visit.

MORE THE PLAYDATE KIDS BOOKS

MUSICAL SERIES CD and Sheet Music Included!

The I Like Me Dance
A visit to the zoo
and a self-esteem boost!

Booger Boogie
A jazzy take on
blowing your nose!

Island Potty Party
A tropical get-together
to learn bathroom skills!

DVD & COLORING BOOK

Behavioral themed
coloring and puzzle book
AND animated cartoon DVD set!

GROWING UP SERIES Guidelines and Activities Included!

Chloe Nova
Chloe gets a new
baby brother!

Cosmos McCool
Cosmos' parents
get a divorce.

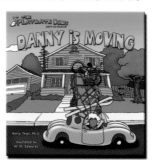

Danny O'Brien
The O'Briens move
to a new house.

Dakota Greenblatt
Dakota's mom goes
to the hospital.

Chloe Nova
Chloe's dog, Marbles,
passes away.

Cosmos McCool
The McCool Family
suddenly grows!

Danny O'Brien
Danny hears a
bad secret.

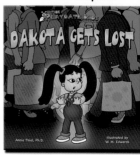

Dakota Greenblatt
Dakota gets lost
at the mall.